GET THAT GHOST TO GO!

by C. MacPhail

illustrated by
Karen Donnelly

Cover illustration by
Brett Hawkins

Librarian Reviewer
Laurie K. Holland
Media Specialist (National Board Certified), Edina, MN
MA in Elementary Education, Minnesota State University, Mankato, MN

Reading Consultant
Elizabeth Stedem
Educator/Consultant, Colorado Springs, CO
MA in Elementary Education, University of Denver, CO

 STONE ARCH BOOKS
Minneapolis   San Diego

j
MAC

First published in the United States in 2006
by Stone Arch Books,
151 Good Counsel Drive, P.O. Box 669,
Mankato, Minnesota 56002.
www.stonearchbooks.com

Published by arrangement with
Barrington Stoke Ltd, Edinburgh.

Library of Congress Cataloging-in-Publication Data
MacPhail, Catherine, 1946–

Get That Ghost to Go! / by C. MacPhail; illustrated by Karen Donnelly.
p. cm.— (Pathway Books)
Summary: When a ghost begins haunting Duncan, turning his life
upside down and ruining his cool image, he and his best friend Markie
turn to the class "nerd," whose plan for getting rid of the ghost comes at
a steep price.
ISBN-13: 978-1-59889-004-4 (hardcover)
ISBN-10: 1-59889-004-2 (hardcover)
ISBN-13: 978-1-59889-195-9 (paperback)
ISBN-10: 1-59889-195-2 (paperback)
[1. Ghosts—Fiction. 2. Popularity—Fiction. 3. Bullies—Fiction.
4. Humorous stories.] I. Donnelly, Karen, ill. II. Title. III. Series.
PZ7.M2426Get 2006
[Fic]—dc22   2005026574

1 2 3 4 5 6 11 10 09 08 07 06

Printed in the United States of America.

TABLE OF CONTENTS

Chapter 1

MARKIE AND ME

One day, Markie and I were playing soccer in the park after school.

Well, Markie was playing soccer. I was leaning against the posts. Markie was playing with the ball. He was showing off to the girls who were standing around watching him.

Girls always watch Markie. He's the best-looking boy in school. At least, that's what he says.

I'm Duncan, and Markie's my best bud. We are what you call 'cool.' We dress cool. We act cool. We are cool.

We aren't on the soccer team. We aren't in a gang. Lots of people want to be our friends, but we don't need them. Some people in school don't even like us! They think we're show-offs, but we aren't. We are just better than everyone else.

Anyway, Markie was bouncing the ball off his head when I heard barking from across the park. I looked over and saw Ross. He was trying to hold back his dogs. They were tugging on their leashes, and they looked really scared.

The dogs were jumping around and yelping. Ross kept tripping as he tried to hold them back.

Ross comes from this odd family that's always taking in stray dogs. I can't tell you how many they have. Their house must be a real mess.

Ross looks like a stray himself. His bright, woolly sweaters are too big for him. His dark hair stands straight up.

Ross wants to be our friend. He waves every time we see him. But Ross . . . a friend of ours? Come on, get real.

Every day, when Ross brought those dogs to the park, they'd act like they were scared of something. I always knew what they'd do. They'd race off and drag Ross around the park on his belly. It was really fun to watch!

That day, I was so busy watching Ross that I didn't see what Markie was doing. He had kicked the ball toward the goal. I turned and saw it coming at me!

"Duncan!" Markie yelled at me.

It was too late. The ball slammed into my face. Everything went black.

When I came to, Markie was bending over me. "Are you all right?" he asked. "Duncan, speak to me!"

I blinked and tried to focus my eyes.

Then the girls came rushing up to us. "Did you hurt yourself?" They asked.

I was just about to reply when I saw that they weren't talking to me. They were talking to Markie.

"I'm the one who was hit!" I told them as Markie helped me stand up. They didn't care about me. They stood around Markie like a fan club. They wanted to be sure he hadn't hurt his foot when he kicked the ball.

I could still hear Ross's dogs yelping. I looked over at them.

Of course they were yelping. A tall, skinny guy with red hair was kicking them. That made me mad. I hate to see animals getting hurt.

"You leave those dogs alone!" I yelled.

This is my idea of fun!

Ross looked over at me. "Me? I haven't touched them."

"Not you. Him!" I pointed at the boy with red hair. I noticed that his clothes were odd. He wore a long, black jacket and tight, black pants. His black shoes had long, pointed toes. Wow! I would hate to be kicked by him!

He looked amazed. "Can you see me?" he asked.

"Of course, I can see you!" I said. "If you kick those dogs one more time, you'll be sorry."

Ross looked at me as if he was going to cry. "Me? I'd never kick my dogs."

"Not you, Ross! Him!" I pointed again to the boy with red hair.

He stuck his tongue out at me. "Make me stop!" he said, and he kicked the dogs again.

That was it! I flung myself at him.

And that's when the most amazing thing happened.

I went right through him!

The dogs rushed off across the park, dragging Ross behind them.

I landed on the grass and yelled, "How did I do that?"

The boy with red hair was jumping around like a wild man.

"Amazing!" he yelled. "You can see me. No one's ever been able to see me before."

"See you?" I said. "What do you mean?"

"Are you stupid?" he asked, bending down over me.

The smell was awful. I saw now that he had one blue eye and one green eye. I was beginning to get really worried about what was happening.

"I'm a ghost," he said softly.

Chapter 2

SPOOKED

I think I blacked out again. When I opened my eyes, Markie was slapping my face.

"Are you okay, pal?" he asked.

"I had an awful dream, Markie," I said. I began to tell it to him, but I saw the tall boy with red hair, black jacket, and pointed shoes. He was standing near Markie, and he was grinning in a very nasty way.

"Can you see him, Markie?"
I pointed at the boy. He was so close I could almost touch his face.

Markie looked around. "Who? Do you mean Ross?" He began to laugh because there was Ross, still being dragged around the park by his dogs.

"Not Ross, him!"

Markie looked to see where my finger was pointing. He was staring right into the boy's face. The boy stuck out his tongue. I waited for Markie to punch him. He wouldn't let the boy get away with that.

Markie looked back at me and said, "No one's there." Then he sniffed. "But there's an awful smell. Is that you?"

The boy jumped up and down.

"No one else can see me! No one else can see me!" He was yelling with joy. "This is going to be fun. I've never haunted a person before."

I grabbed Markie's arm. "You have to see that boy," I said. "If you can't, it means he really is a . . ."

But how could he be a ghost? He was as solid as Markie and me. He looked just like a normal boy, except for a green glow all around him — and that smell.

"He's a what?" Markie asked.

It was hard to get the words out. "He's a ghost."

"I'm a ghost!" the boy yelled. "My name's Dean. If I'm going to haunt you, you should know my name."

"He says his name's Dean, and he's going to haunt me."

Markie looked worried. "It's that bump on the head from the soccer ball. That's why you're seeing things. I'm going to take you home."

"I'm coming, too," Dean said.

"No!" I yelled.

"I'm only trying to help you, Duncan," Markie exclaimed.

"I'm not talking to you." I shouted at Markie. "I'm talking to him."

If there's one thing about Markie, it's this — he's the best friend you could ever have. At least, that's what he says.

"If you say there's a ghost, then there's a ghost. You wouldn't lie to me." Markie stood up.

"So where is he? I'll take care of him," said Markie.

He was ready for a fight, and Markie is the best fighter in the school. At least, that's what he says. But I've never seen him fight with anyone. He just makes them laugh, and that's it.

Markie held up his fists and began to jump around like a boxer. "Now, tell me where this ghost is. I'm going to punch him out!"

Poor Markie didn't have a chance of winning this one. I watched in horror as Dean breathed in and then blew out so hard that Markie was lifted off his feet and thrown across the park.

I jumped to my feet. "You're evil!" I yelled at Dean.

Dean made a stupid face. "I'm a ghost. You think I'm going to be nice?"

I ran over to Markie. He was lying in a bush. He had mud all over him.

"Was that the ghost?" he asked.

"Yeah, it was," I said.

Markie looked around. "Is he still here?"

He was there all right, standing right behind Markie.

Markie sniffed. The smell was awful, like rotting fish. "I think I can smell him."

Dean didn't like that. He kicked Markie on the shin. Then he sat down on the grass and stared at his pointed shoes.

"Hope that kick didn't hurt my boots," he said. "They're cool, don't you think?"

I thought his pointed shoes looked stupid, but I didn't say that.

Markie was holding his shin. "I thought ghosts couldn't hurt you."

"I can," Dean said. "I can kick and punch, and no one can see me. It's fun being a ghost."

"Remember I can see you now," I told him.

"I know, and that's going to be fun, too. You're never going to get rid of me, Duncan," said Dean.

Chapter 3

OVER MY DEAD BODY

Markie phoned me that night. "Is the ghost still there?"

"He's still here," I said. In fact, Dean was sitting on my bed. The smell was awful. "My mom's not happy at all. She says something smells funny."

"Of course I smell funny," Dean said. "I've been dead for more than 50 years."

I tried to ignore him.

I pulled the blanket over my head and spoke softly into the phone. "My mom thinks I've got a dead cat in here. And the ghost is making a mess."

He was, too. He had thrown my video games everywhere. He had pulled my clothes out of the drawers and scattered them around the room.

"Mom's going to kill me when she sees what he's done."

"I'm coming over to see you," Markie told me.

A little while later, when Markie stepped into the room, Dean tripped him. Markie landed in a pile of my dirty laundry.

"Where is he?" yelled Markie. "I'm going to get him this time."

Markie jumped up and was turning this way and that. So was Dean. One moment he was in front of Markie, punching his nose, and the next he was behind him, kicking him in the backside.

Dean thought it was funny.

"But I came here with a plan to help him," Markie cried.

"What's your plan?" Dean and I said at the same time.

"It's a great plan," Markie said.

It had to be a great plan. Markie is the smartest boy in school. At least, that's what he says.

"We're going to help him rest in peace," Markie said.

"How?" Dean and I asked at the same time.

"How did Dean die? Ask him if it was murder," said Markie. "Does he want us to find out who did it and put them in prison?"

Dean shook his head. "It wasn't murder."

I told this to Markie.

"Maybe there was something he wanted to do before he died that he wants us to do for him," Markie said. "Did he want to tell someone that he loved them or something like that?"

"What a stupid idea!" Dean said, and laughed.

"He says that's a stupid idea,"
I told Markie.

"I'm only trying to help," Markie
said. "How did he die anyway?"

Dean thought for a moment. "I
can't remember," he said. "It was a
long time ago."

"He can't remember how he died," I
told Markie.

Markie didn't believe him. "You
can't forget something like that."

Dean was trying to think. "I
remember I had a firecracker in my
hand, and I was chasing a dog with
it. That dog was really scared. I was
having a great time! That's the last
thing I remember."

When I told Markie what Dean had said, Markie went crazy!

"If that's why he's a ghost," he said, "I don't even know why we're trying to help him."

Dean came up very close to Markie and blew air at him. Markie's face turned green. I thought he was going to faint. "That ghost stinks!" he said.

Dean blew Markie right off the bed. Then he turned to me and said, "You tell your pal, Markie, that I don't want any help. I like being a ghost. It's even more fun now that you can see me."

When I told Markie this, he stood up. "Okay, Duncan, that's it," he said. "We're going to get rid of that ghost."

Dean couldn't stop laughing.

"Over my dead body!" he said, and laughed so hard he fell off the bed. "Get the joke? Over my dead body!"

Chapter 4

HELP! I'M STUCK WITH A GHOST!

Dean was still sitting on my bed when I woke up the next morning. He still smelled awful.

"What is that smell, Duncan?" my mom asked me at breakfast. "Is it your feet?"

That made Dean laugh so hard he pulled the cloth off the table. The plates and cups crashed onto the floor.

I got blamed for that, too.

* * *

"We've got to get that ghost to go," I told Markie when I met him at the school gates.

"Is he with you now?" asked Markie.

In reply, Dean tripped him, and Markie fell flat on his face in a puddle. Someone behind us was laughing at him.

"Look at the cool guy!" It was Sunna, the only girl in school who didn't like Markie. "Not so cool now, are you, Markie?"

Markie frowned at her. I think he likes Sunna, but of course, he'd never say that. I helped him get up. Markie gave me a look.

"We've just got to get that ghost to go!" he said.

Sunna walked off, laughing.

"She doesn't like Markie much, does she?" Dean was pleased about that. His one green eye and his one blue eye had a wicked gleam in them.

"I could make her like him even less." Dean stuck out his foot and tripped her. Now she was the one who went face down in a puddle.

Sunna was back on her feet at once. She was very angry. She looked right at Markie.

"It wasn't me!" he yelled at her. But she didn't believe him. She ran at him, swung him round three times, and sent him spinning into the bushes.

Markie never looked so uncool.

He was in a very bad mood when we went into class. Everyone had seen what Sunna did to him, and they were all laughing at him. Markie and I weren't used to that, and it was all Dean's fault. He was sitting beside me in class, grinning.

I didn't understand why no one else could see him. He looked as solid as me. But he did have this green glow around him, and he smelled.

Everyone was moving away from me and sniffing.

"You smell disgusting," Sunna said in a loud voice.

Mr. Barr, our teacher, looked up. He was sniffing, too. "Have you got a dead dog in your bag, Duncan?" he asked. Then Mr. Barr laughed until his toupee wobbled.

"Did he say I smelled like a dead dog?" Dean asked.

"You do smell like a dead dog," I told him.

It was my bad luck that Mr. Barr thought I was saying it to him.

"Come here, Duncan!" he said.

I walked up to his desk with Dean right behind me.

"You do smell awful!" Mr. Barr said, and he held his nose. That made Dean mad.

"I'm going to make him sorry he said that," he told me.

"Shut up!" I yelled. Dean was getting me into real trouble.

"What did you say?" asked Mr. Barr, getting more and more angry.

"I didn't mean you, sir," I told him.

Then, to my horror, Dean snatched Mr. Barr's toupee right off his head. I tried to stop him, and of course, what did it look like?

It looked as if I was the one who had taken off his toupee.

Mr. Barr was yelling at me. He had his hands over his bald head. The class was going crazy. Dean threw the toupee across the room. It hit Markie in the face.

"So you two are in this together! Now you're both in deep trouble!" said Mr. Barr.

We were sent off to the principal's office. Dean danced after us. He was enjoying every minute.

Markie and I looked at each other.

"We've got to get that ghost to go!" we both said.

Chapter 5

ENTER GREG

The principal yelled at us for hours. Dean made things worse by knocking all of the papers off his desk. We got blamed for that. Then he spilled coffee down the principal's shirt. We got blamed for that, too.

It just wasn't fair.

"Were you this bad when you were still alive?" Markie asked Dean as we walked home.

"Hey, look at the cool guys," Sunna shouted so everyone could hear her. "They're talking to someone who's not even there."

Everyone was laughing at Markie and me. We're not used to that.

Greg was the only one who didn't laugh. Greg's the school nerd. He'd rather read a book than go to the movies. And he uses his computer to research science stuff instead of playing games. He looks just like Harry Potter — floppy hair and glasses. All he needs is the scar.

Greg was looking at us now. He walked over to me and Markie. "It seems to me that you and your friend are acting in a very odd manner," he said.

Greg always talks like that. No wonder he annoys everyone.

"There must be a reason why you two are acting so oddly," Greg went on. "And I ask myself what that reason could be. Would you like to tell me what's going on?"

My eyes lit up. I turned to Markie.

"Markie," I said, "this could be just what we need. Greg is really smart. He knows everything. He could help us."

Then I added, too softly for Dean to hear, "He could help us get this ghost to go."

Markie wasn't sure.

"He's a nerd, Duncan. We can't be seen with someone like Greg."

Dean came closer to Markie and me. "What are you two whispering about?" he asked.

Greg came closer to us, too. Really close. His face turned green.

"What's that awful smell?" he asked.

Dean sniffed under his arms. "It's not me that's smelly. And I don't like you saying that it is."

Then he hit Greg on the nose. Markie grabbed him just as he fell.

"Who did that?" Greg asked.

"You won't believe us," I said.

"Try me," said Greg.

So we told him everything.

We told him how I first saw Dean just after my bump on the head. We told him that he was still there, but I was the only person who could see him. We told him Dean wanted to haunt me forever.

"It sounds as if the bump on the head made it possible for you to see ghosts. Things like that do happen," Greg said.

He nodded his head very wisely. His nose was still bleeding.

"You say he dresses funny?" Greg asked.

"Dresses funny!" That made Dean mad. "Everyone thinks I'm cool!"

"He thinks he's cool," I told Greg.

Greg nodded. "I've read about guys like him," he said. "They wore tight, black pants and long, pointed shoes called winkle-pickers. And they were 'cool' in their day. Myself, I always thought they looked stupid."

Dean's reply was to punch Greg in the nose again.

"I could help you get rid of him," Greg said as he wiped more blood from his nose. He looked angry now.

"Do you think so?" Dean snarled as he kicked Greg in the ankle.

Greg yelped.

"He's driving us nuts, Greg. So how are you going to help us get rid of him?" I asked.

"You'll never get rid of me," Dean said. "You're stuck with me forever."

Then he grinned. That made him look really scary. His face turned green, and his teeth were blacker than ever.

Was I stuck with him forever? What a horrible idea! "Greg! You've got to help us. We've got to get that ghost to go!"

"All right," said Greg. "I'll help you. But only if you do something for me."

Chapter 6

FROM WORSE TO EVEN WORSE!

Then Greg told us what he wanted, but it was not what we thought it would be.

He didn't want money. He didn't want Markie to get him a girlfriend. He just wanted to be cool. He told us he was fed up with being a nerd.

Greg wanted to be our friend.

That was a tough request. Greg was the kind of guy we tried to stay away from. He wasn't normal. He even did his homework! But we had no choice. So we said he could be our friend, and Greg said he would help us.

He was going to find out all he could to help us get rid of Dean.

Dean was right behind me all the way home. He kicked a dog, and it yelped, and I got the blame. The owner was Mrs. Todd who lives on our street, and she said she was going to phone my mom. So Dean kicked her, too.

Mrs. Todd grabbed me by the ear and dragged me home.

Boy, was my mom mad!

"Kicking Mrs. Todd's dog! And then kicking Mrs. Todd! I'm ashamed of you, Duncan," she said.

"But, Mom —" I kept trying to explain.

She wouldn't let me say a word.

She only sniffed. "And as for those feet, they stink! Go take a bath."

The bad thing was that Dean stayed in the bathroom with me the whole time. He sat on the toilet and talked about how much he enjoyed being a ghost and how he would never leave me.

I phoned Markie from my bedroom.

"I'm going crazy. I don't care if Greg is a nerd. He can marry my sister if he helps us!"

"But think what this will do to us, Duncan. If we let Greg be our friend, we won't look cool anymore," Markie said.

"It's okay for you," I replied. "You don't have an ugly ghost sitting on your bed. No one thinks you smell."

I knew Markie would help me. He was a true friend.

"Okay, pal. I'll call Greg and see if he's got a plan."

I put down the phone. Dean looked angry. "Did you call me ugly?" he said.

"Yeah, you are ugly. Look in the mirror."

Dean was so mad that he pulled out all of my drawers again and threw my clothes all over the floor.

I jumped off the bed and yelled, "Stop that!"

My mom came rushing into the room just as Dean was pushing the books off the shelf, and I was trying to stop him.

"What is wrong with you, Duncan? Why are you shouting like that? And look at this mess!"

"It wasn't me, Mom," I tried to tell her. But why would she believe me? Who else could have done it?

"You're telling me there's someone in here I can't see?" she asked.

She held her nose.

"And if that smell isn't gone by the weekend," she said, "I'm taking you to the doctor. Even a boy's feet can't smell that bad."

I lay down on the bed after she left the room. Things were going from bad to worse.

Dean was sitting in a corner, laughing and laughing.

I wasn't laughing at all. I knew then for sure. I had to get that ghost to go.

Chapter 7

WE'VE GOT TO GET THAT GHOST TO GO!

For the first time in my life, I was excited to go to school. I didn't sleep all night because Dean was sitting on my bed, and he never stopped talking.

"Well, I've had no one to talk to for years. Can you blame me?" he said.

I pulled the blanket over my head, but that awful smell was still there. It was like rotting fish, and it was getting worse every day.

"You look awful, Duncan," Markie said to me when he saw me at school.

He was right. I looked in the mirror that morning — white face, black eyes, and my hair standing on end. I looked more like a ghost than Dean did.

Greg came running over to us. "Hi, guys!" he shouted. I could see most of our class watching him. Were Greg, Markie and I pals now? Something was wrong.

"Have you got a plan?" I asked him.

"What plan?" Dean said.

Greg nodded. "We are going to get rid of him."

"Do you know how to do it?" Markie and I gasped.

"I went to the library last night. I read every book I could about ghosts and why they haunt people. This one just seems to enjoy it." Greg was proud of what he had done.

Dean laughed. "He's got that right," he said. "I love haunting people."

Greg went on talking. "And I read about how to get ghosts to go, too. You have to EX-OR-CISE them. That's how you get rid of a ghost."

Markie hugged Greg as if he'd just scored a goal. "You're brilliant, Greg!" he shouted.

I hugged them both. "What a guy!"

The whole school was looking at us now. But Markie and I didn't care if we didn't look cool. We didn't care if people thought Greg was our friend. The whole ghost thing had been too much for us.

Dean stood there watching.

"What's Greg talking about?" Dean asked us.

It was lucky that Dean was such a stupid ghost. He had no idea what we were up to.

He gave us a headache that day, Markie, Greg and me.

Dean tipped over Greg's class project, which included a jar full of frogs. They jumped around everywhere. It had taken Greg weeks to collect them, and now he was in tears.

Then Dean locked the science teacher in the closet with the frogs and threw away the key. She was in there for an hour, crying and shouting, and it was Greg who got the blame.

"We've got to get that ghost to go!" he wailed.

At lunchtime, Dean pushed Markie's head into his plate of food just when he was trying to show Sunna how cool he was. It's very hard to look good with mashed potatoes all over your face.

Sunna walked away, laughing with all of her friends, and Markie wailed, "We've got to get that ghost to go!"

In the boys' bathroom, Dean locked Big Harry, the biggest boy in the school, in one of the stalls.

Who do you think got blamed? Me. I was the only other person in there, so who else could have done it? And what did I get in return? Big Harry pushed my head in a toilet and flushed it.

He said it might get rid of the smell.

The smell was everywhere. By the end of the day I was put in a corner of the classroom, away from everyone. Not everyone, of course. Dean was there, right beside me, grinning.

I had only one thought in my head. We've got to get that ghost to go!

Chapter 8

GOING, GOING, GONE

After school, the three of us — Greg, Markie, and me — went over to the park. Greg said we had to go to the place where I first saw Dean. That was where we had to get rid of him.

I say the three of us, but it was really the four of us. Dean was with us the whole time.

"Where are we going?" he asked.

When Dean saw we were getting near the park, he started to jump around. "I love going to the park! Now, where's that stupid Ross and his stray dogs? I hate those animals! I would hate to live in his house."

Just then Ross came around a corner. He had six of his dogs with him. As soon as they saw Dean they started to growl and bark.

"Look!" yelled Dean. "They're scared of me! This is great!" And then he got ready to kick those poor dogs again.

The dogs saw him coming and yelped. They pulled Ross right off his feet. Then they were off with Dean right after them.

"Come back here!" I yelled to Dean.

But he didn't hear me. He was having too much fun.

"Where is he now?" Greg asked.

"Chasing Ross and his dogs. Look!" I said.

It was funny. I couldn't help laughing. Ross was being dragged along by the dogs. He was trying to hold them back. Of course, Dean gave Ross a few kicks as he ran past.

"We can't get rid of Dean if he's not here," yelled Greg. "Get him back!"

We had to wait until Dean and Ross and the dogs ran all the way around the park and came back. It was Markie and me who grabbed Ross and stopped him and his dogs from running past us again.

"Do you want your dogs to stop dragging you around the park every day?" I asked.

Ross nodded.

"Then tie them to a tree and do just what we do," I told him.

We had to work hard to tie up those dogs. They didn't want to stay. They were going wild.

Dean thought we were trying to help him. "Thanks, boys," he said. "Now I can scare them, and they can't even run away."

I felt sorry for the poor dogs. "It won't be for long," I told them.

"This will work, won't it?" Markie asked Greg.

"Of course!" Greg said. Then he added, "Well, I hope it will. Now, do everything I do."

He started saying a really weird chant.

"I don't know what he's doing," Markie said. Greg told him to shut up and join in. So he did. Greg's eyes crossed. All our eyes crossed. Then Greg began to dance.

"Is he sick?" Ross asked.

Greg began to chant again. This time we could hear the words.

"We've got to get that ghost to go!"

"We've got to get that ghost to go!"

I joined in:

"We've got to get that ghost to go!"

Then Markie joined in, too. Only he was singing it as if it were a rap song:

"We've got to get that ghost to go!"

"We've got to get that ghost to go!"

"We've got to get that ghost."

"We've got to get that ghost."

"We've got to get that ghost to go!"

Greg was angry. "This isn't a joke," he said.

But no one listened to him. I liked the rap, so I started singing it that way, too. So did Ross.

Soon the beat got to Greg, and he started to dance and sing with the rest of us. We must have looked odd.

Even Dean joined in. He started dancing and singing, too.

"We've got to get that ghost to go!"

"We've got to get that ghost to go!"

"We've got to get that —"

Suddenly, Dean stopped singing. "Are you trying to get rid of me?" he asked.

I told you he was dumb.

But we didn't stop singing, and Dean began to look worried.

"I feel funny," he said.

"It's working!" I shouted. "Keep singing!"

Dean was fading, a little at a time. First his feet and then his legs.

"Hey! Where are my legs?"

By the time Dean shouted that, he had vanished up to his stomach.

He knew he was fading, and there was nothing he could do to stop it. But he gave me a wicked grin.

"You won't get rid of me!"

Then there was only his face, an angry face. Before long, all that was left was his voice, an angry voice.

"I'll be back!" Dean warned me.

His words drifted through the air and made me shiver.

The dogs stopped yelping, and their tails started wagging.

"He's gone, isn't he?" Markie yelled.

"He says he'll come back, and I bet he will," I said.

Greg nodded. "Yeah, I bet he will, too. But not as a ghost. He'll come back as something else."

"What?" I asked.

Just then the dogs began barking again and pulling at their leashes.

"What's the matter with them now?" Markie asked.

Then we saw an ugly cat watching us from the bushes. A skinny, orange cat. It arched its back, showed its teeth, and spat at the dogs.

Ross picked it up. "Poor little thing," he said, and he tried to stroke it.

The "poor little thing" scratched Ross as it tried to get away.

I looked at Greg. "You don't think it could be . . . ?"

Greg bent down over the cat. "Do you think it's Dean?"

The cat spat and sprang at him.

The cat sank its claws into Greg's face and didn't let go. It took all of us to pull its claws free.

Then the cat jumped down and ran off. The dogs were after it in a flash.

"If that cat is Dean," I said, "I don't feel sorry for it at all. Dean was always chasing those dogs. Now they're getting even with him."

Greg had scratches all over his face. "It's Dean all right," he said. "It has one green eye and one blue eye."

Markie jumped in the air.

"We did it!" He hugged me. "We did it!"

I hugged him, too, and then we both jumped on Greg. "We did it!"

Ross didn't understand what it was all about, but he jumped on the rest of us. "We did it!" he yelled. Then he shook his head. "What did we do?"

Chapter 9

TOTALLY COOL

Did things go back to normal after that? No! Everything changed.

We had to stay friends with Greg. He saved us. And we said we'd teach him to be cool. But we didn't have to because when the orange cat scratched Greg's face it left a great big scar.

Now Greg really does look like Harry Potter, and that makes him look totally cool.

Anyway, it's not all that important to be cool now. You see, Dean thought he was cool, and there is no way Markie and I want to be like Dean.

Markie and Sunna are always together now, and someone has written *Markie loves Sunna* in the boys' bathroom.

I always had a funny feeling that Markie liked Sunna. Sunna says she started to like Markie when she saw him with mashed potatoes all over his face.

"But I looked stupid," Markie said.

"I know. But I think I like you that way," she said.

Ross is our friend now, too. He waits for us at the park every day.

Ross even comes with us to the movies on weekends. Funny thing is, he's really fun. I don't know why we didn't let him be our friend before.

Ross kept the orange cat. He took it home to live with all the other strays.

"Well, we've only got dogs," Ross said, "and I've always wanted a cat."

He even calls the cat Dean. And almost every day I see it being chased by one of Ross's dogs.

Dean always said he would hate to live in Ross's house with all those dogs. Now his nightmare has come true.

And me?

Well, I haven't seen another ghost.

Or have I?

Dean looked like a normal boy. He looked as real as Markie and me.

So how do I know if I've seen another ghost or not?

How do *you* know?

You could meet one on the street and not even know it.

Or you could be standing next to one at the bus stop.

Or sitting beside one at the movies.

They could be all around you, and you don't even know it.

There could be a ghost sitting beside you right now.

It makes you think . . .

ABOUT THE AUTHOR

Catherine MacPhail always wanted to be a writer, but as a child she lacked confidence. Now Catherine writes books and stories for people of all ages. She also has her own comedy radio show.

Catherine always uses real people in her stories and writes about situations from real life.

GLOSSARY

exorcise (EKS-or-size)—to get rid of an evil spirit

haunt (HAWNT)—to constantly visit a place or bother someone

shin (SHIN)—the front part of the leg below the knee

stray (STRAY)—an animal that is lost or without an owner, such as a stray dog

toupee (too-PAY)—a small wig worn to cover a man's bald head

vanish (VAN-ish)—to disappear

yelp (YELP)—a loud bark or cry

DISCUSSION QUESTIONS

1. Dean the ghost was mean to everyone he met. Why do you think he treated everyone so badly?

2. Sunna didn't like Markie when he acted cool. Why do you think she liked him at the end of the story? Explain.

3. Greg helped Duncan and Markie get rid of the ghost. What do you think would have happened if they had been "too cool" to accept his help?

WRITING PROMPTS

1. Duncan probably didn't believe in ghosts until he saw one. What about you? Write and explain why you do or don't believe in ghosts.

2. Sometimes good things happen because of bad experiences. Because of the ghost, Duncan and Markie made new friends. Write about a time when something bad happened to you, but something good came out of it.

3. Imagine that you are a ghost. Write about how you would haunt people.

INTERNET SITES

Do you want to know more about subjects related to this book? Or are you interested in learning about other topics? Then check out FactHound, a fun, easy way to find Internet sites.

Our investigative staff has already sniffed out great sites for you!

Here's how to use FactHound:

1. Visit *www.facthound.com*

2. Select your grade level.

3. To learn more about subjects related to this book, type in the book's ISBN number: **1598890042**.

4 Click the **Fetch It** button.

FactHound will fetch the best Internet sites for you.